PEACE
AND QUIET

DISCARDED

Brigitte **LUCIANI** & Eve **THARLET**

Graphic Universe™ • Minneapolis • New York

For Louise and Loly, for summertime friends . . .
—E.T.

Story by Brigitte Luciani

Art by Eve Tharlet

Translation by Carol Klio Burrell

First American edition published in 2012 by Graphic Universe™.
Published by arrangement with MEDIATOON LICENSING - France.

Monsieur Blaireau et Madame Renarde
4/Jamais tranquille!
© DARGAUD 2010 - Tharlet & Luciani
www.dargaud.com

English translation copyright © 2012 by Lerner Publishing Group, Inc.

Graphic Universe™ is a trademark of Lerner Publishing Group, Inc.

All worldwide English-language rights reserved. No part of this book may
be reproduced, stored in a retrieval system, or transmitted in any form
or by any means—electronic, mechanical, photocopying, recording, or otherwise—
without the prior written permission of Lerner Publishing Group, Inc., except
for the inclusion of brief quotations in an acknowledged review.

Graphic Universe™
A division of Lerner Publishing Group, Inc.
241 First Avenue North
Minneapolis, MN 55401 U.S.A.

Website address: www.lernerbooks.com

Library of Congress Cataloging-in-Publication Data

Luciani, Brigitte.
 [Jamais tranquille! English]
 Peace and quiet / by Brigitte Luciani ; illustrated by Eve Tharlet.
    p.   cm. — (Mr. Badger and Mrs. Fox ; 4)
 Summary: Despite their different habits, Mr. Badger and Mrs. Fox
    get their blended family ready for winter.
 ISBN 978-0-7613-8520-2 (lib. bdg. : alk. paper)
 1. Graphic novels. [1. Graphic novels. 2. Stepfamilies—Fiction. 3. Brothers and sisters—
Fiction. 4. Badgers—Fiction. 5. Foxes—Fiction. 6. Winter—Fiction.] I. Tharlet, Eve, ill. II. Title.
 PZ7.7.L83Pe 2012
 741.5'944—dc23   2011049904

Manufactured in the United States of America
1 - DP - 7/15/12

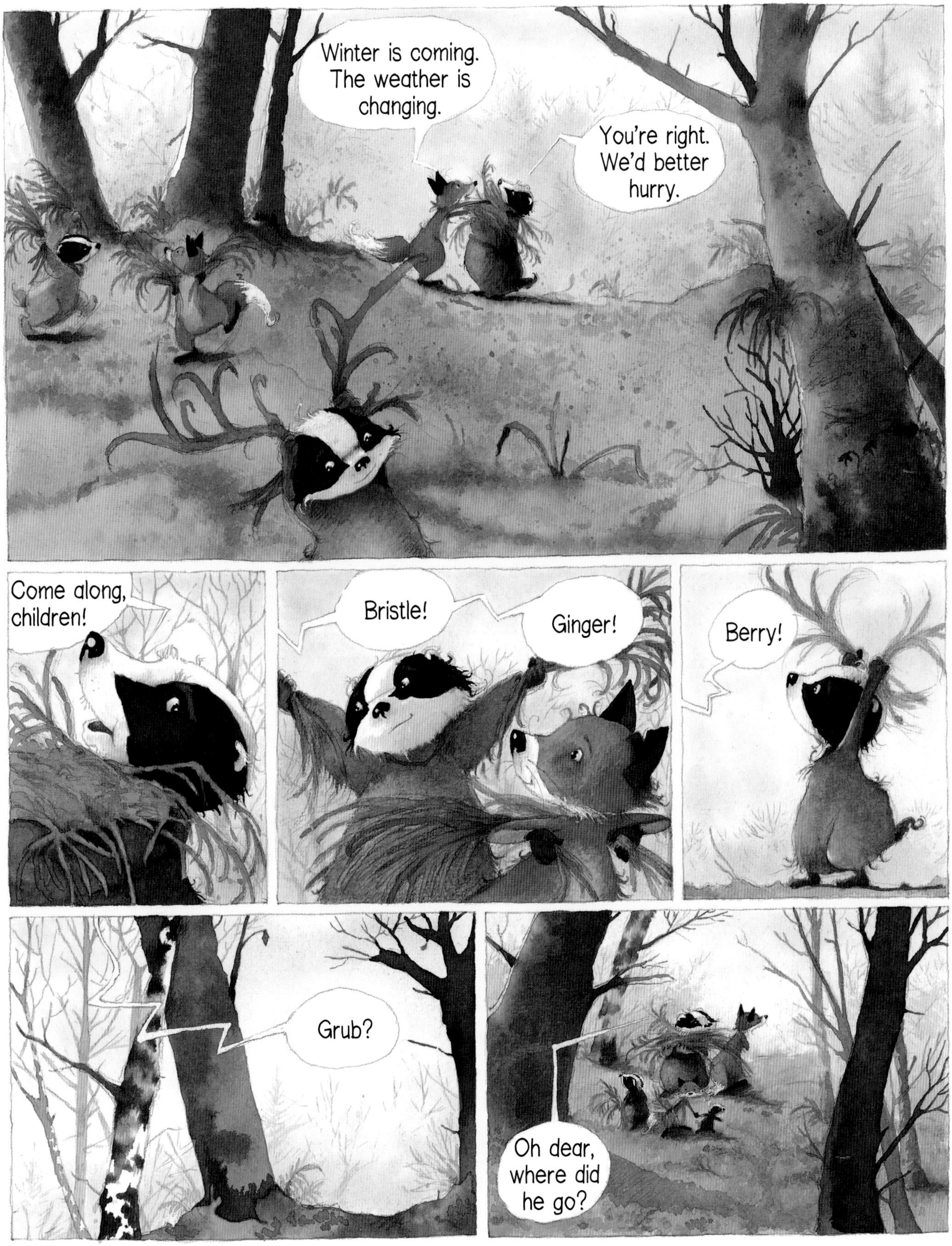
Winter is coming. The weather is changing.
You're right. We'd better hurry.
Come along, children!
Bristle!
Ginger!
Berry!
Grub?
Oh dear, where did he go?

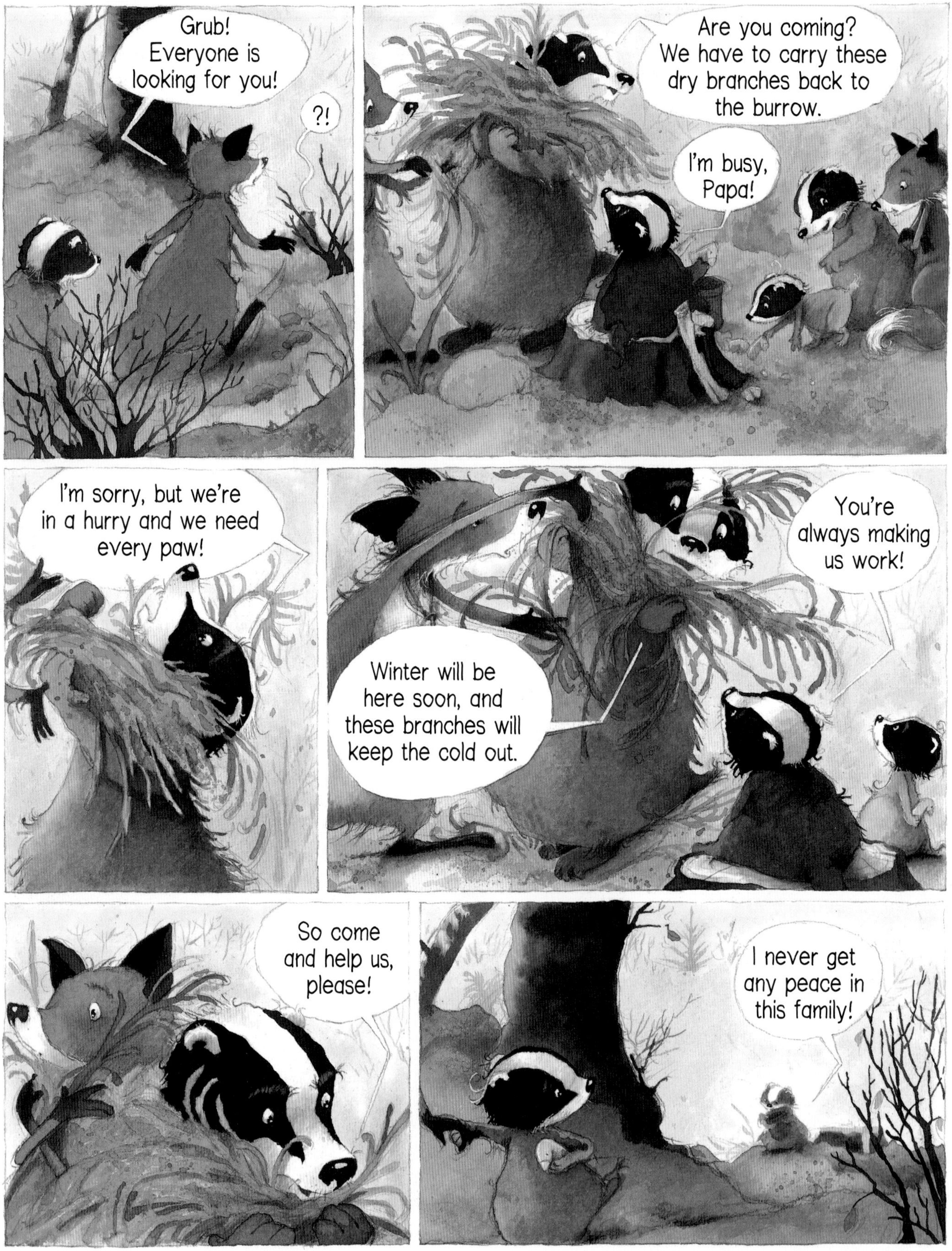
Grub! Everyone is looking for you!
?!
Are you coming? We have to carry these dry branches back to the burrow.
I'm busy, Papa!
I'm sorry, but we're in a hurry and we need every paw!
You're always making us work!
Winter will be here soon, and these branches will keep the cold out.
So come and help us, please!
I never get any peace in this family!

With a hothead like Ginger, we'll be overheated!

Now that we all live together, I'm not worried about being cold.

The more of us there are, the warmer we'll be.

Chin up, Grub!

During the winter, you'll have no work to do. Sometimes for whole weeks!

Hurrah for winter!

Hard work should be rewarded!

Who's hungry?

Me!

AGAIN?!

Berry!

Uh... me!

6

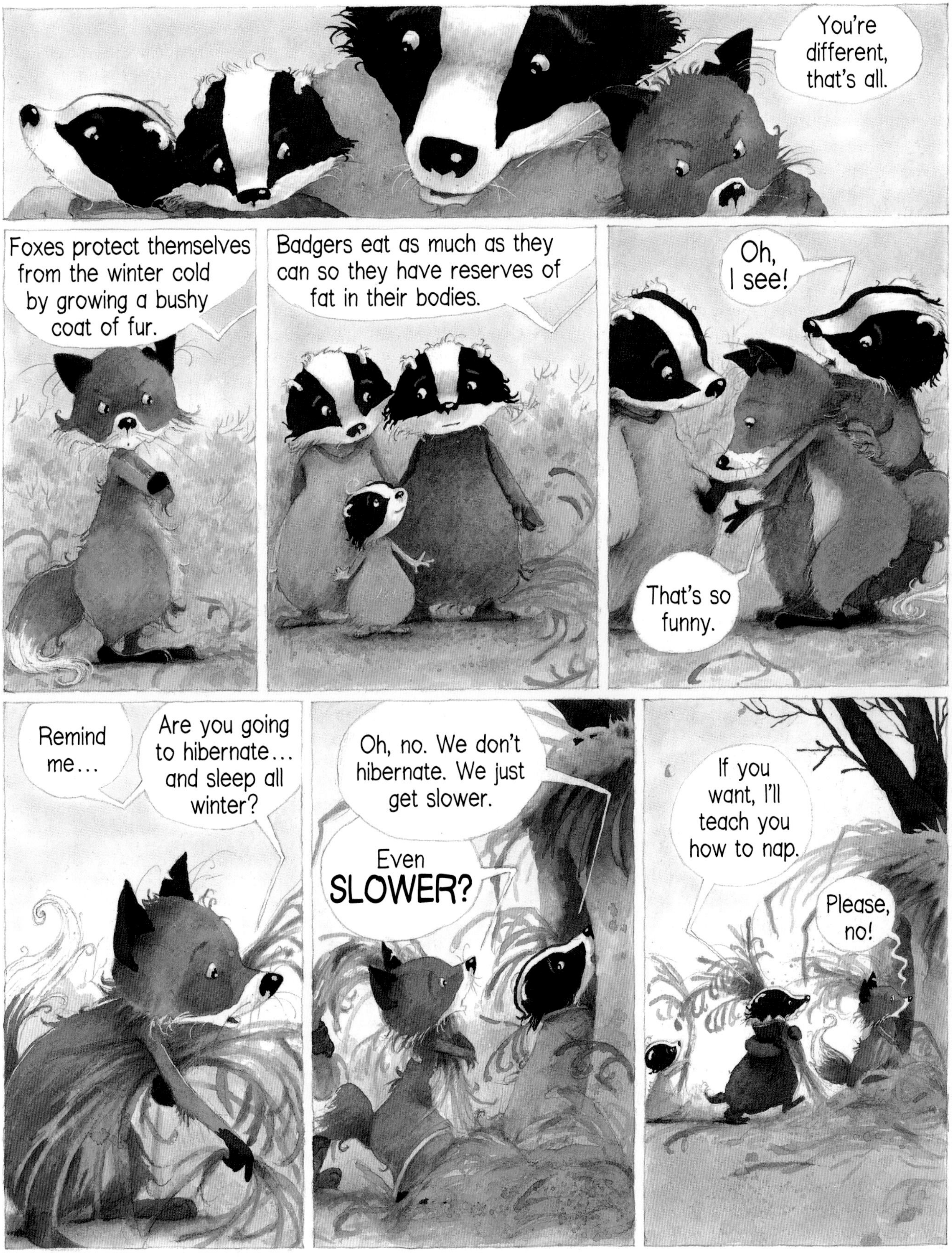

You're different, that's all.
Foxes protect themselves from the winter cold by growing a bushy coat of fur.
Badgers eat as much as they can so they have reserves of fat in their bodies.
Oh, I see!
That's so funny.
Remind me…
Are you going to hibernate… and sleep all winter?
Oh, no. We don't hibernate. We just get slower.
Even SLOWER?
If you want, I'll teach you how to nap.
Please, no!

But since we're all cooped up in here together, things might get less peaceful soon...

Don't worry. We always just sleep a lot.

You, maybe. But not us!

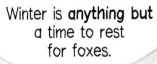

Winter is **anything but** a time to rest for foxes.

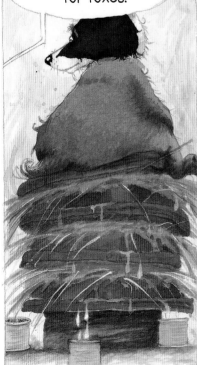

Then just enjoy this moment of quiet!

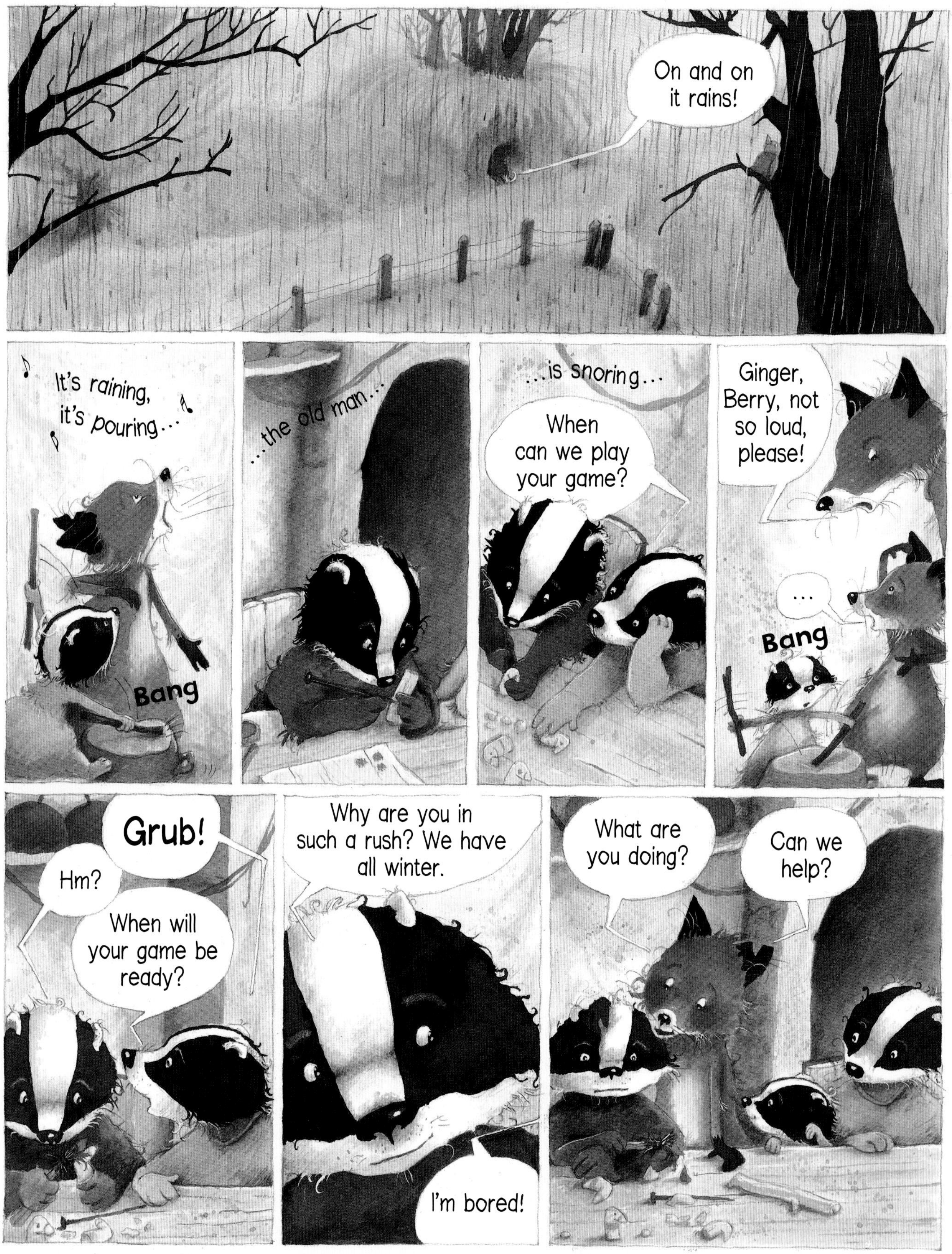

On and on it rains!
It's raining, it's pouring...
Bang
...the old man...
...is snoring...
When can we play your game?
Ginger, Berry, not so loud, please!
...
Bang
Grub!
Hm?
When will your game be ready?
Why are you in such a rush? We have all winter.
I'm bored!
What are you doing?
Can we help?

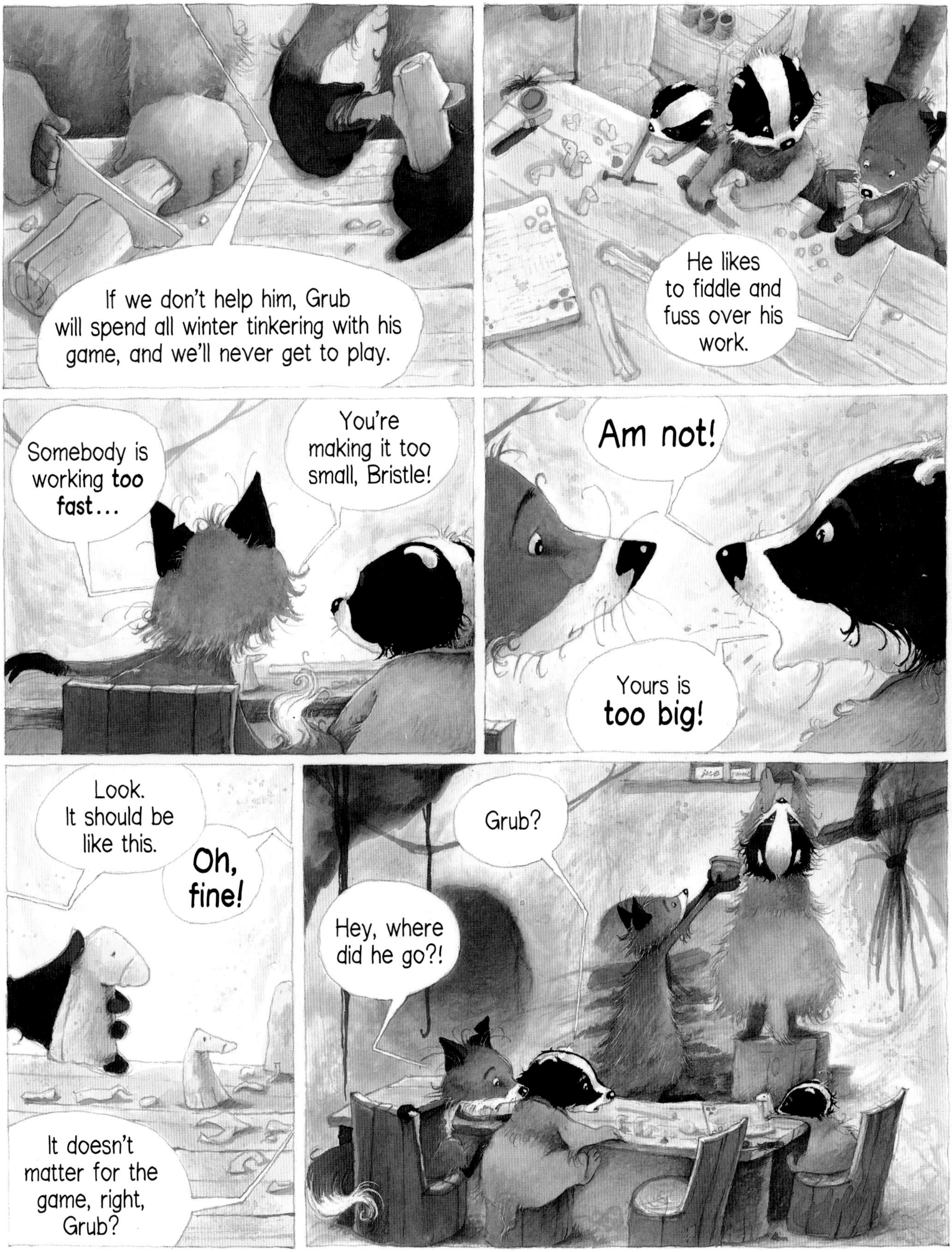
If we don't help him, Grub will spend all winter tinkering with his game, and we'll never get to play.
He likes to fiddle and fuss over his work.
Somebody is working **too fast**...
You're making it too small, Bristle!
Am not!
Yours is **too big!**
Look. It should be like this.
Oh, fine!
It doesn't matter for the game, right, Grub?
Grub?
Hey, where did he go?!

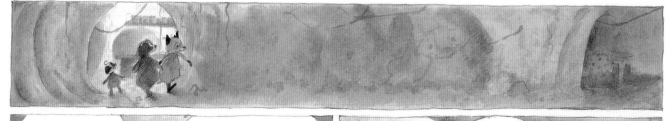

Unbelievable!

We're working while his lordship is sleeping!

Nap time's over!

Hm?

What's up?

We need you! The game is ready.

You need to tell us the rules.

Never a moment's peace!

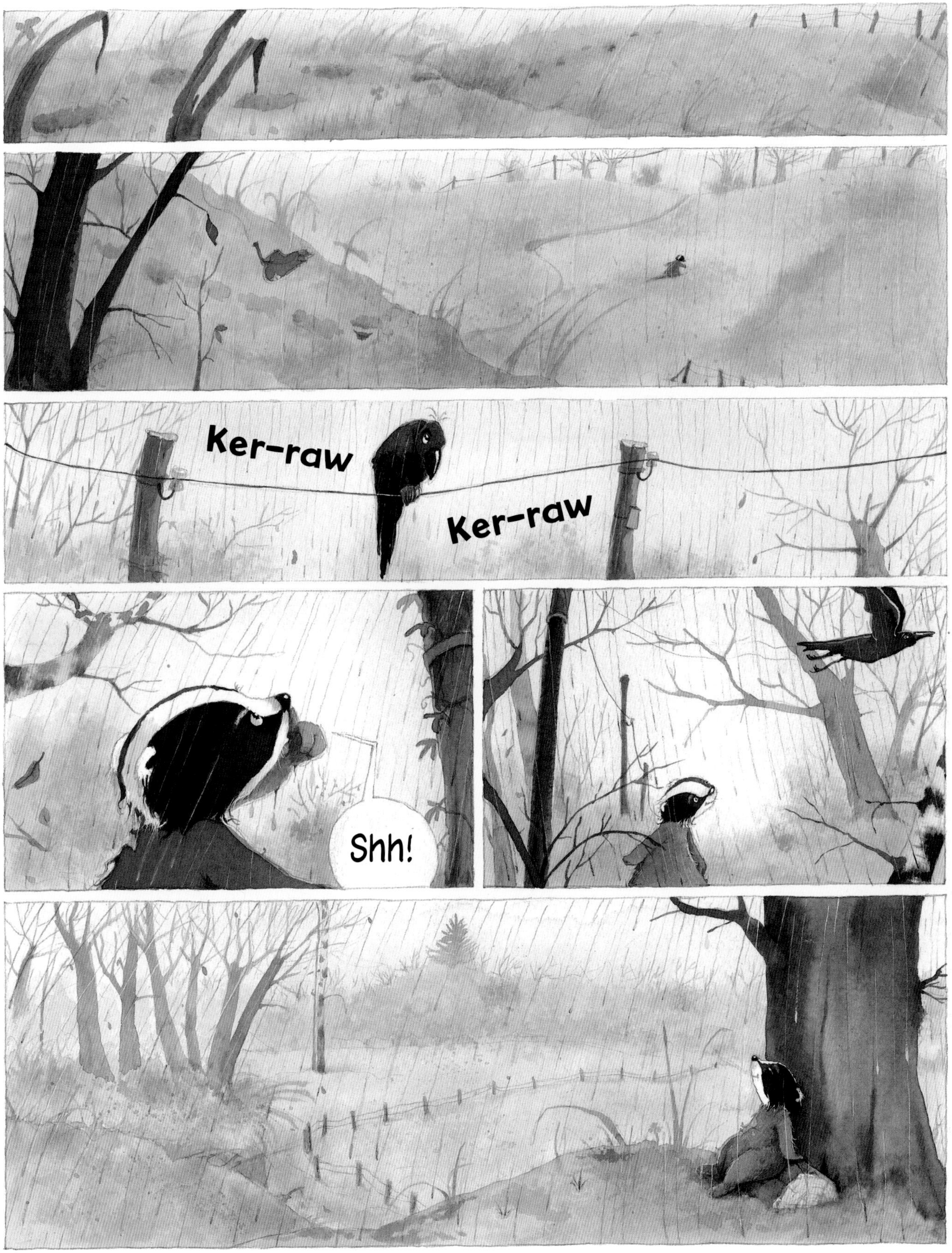
Ker-raw
Ker-raw
Shh!

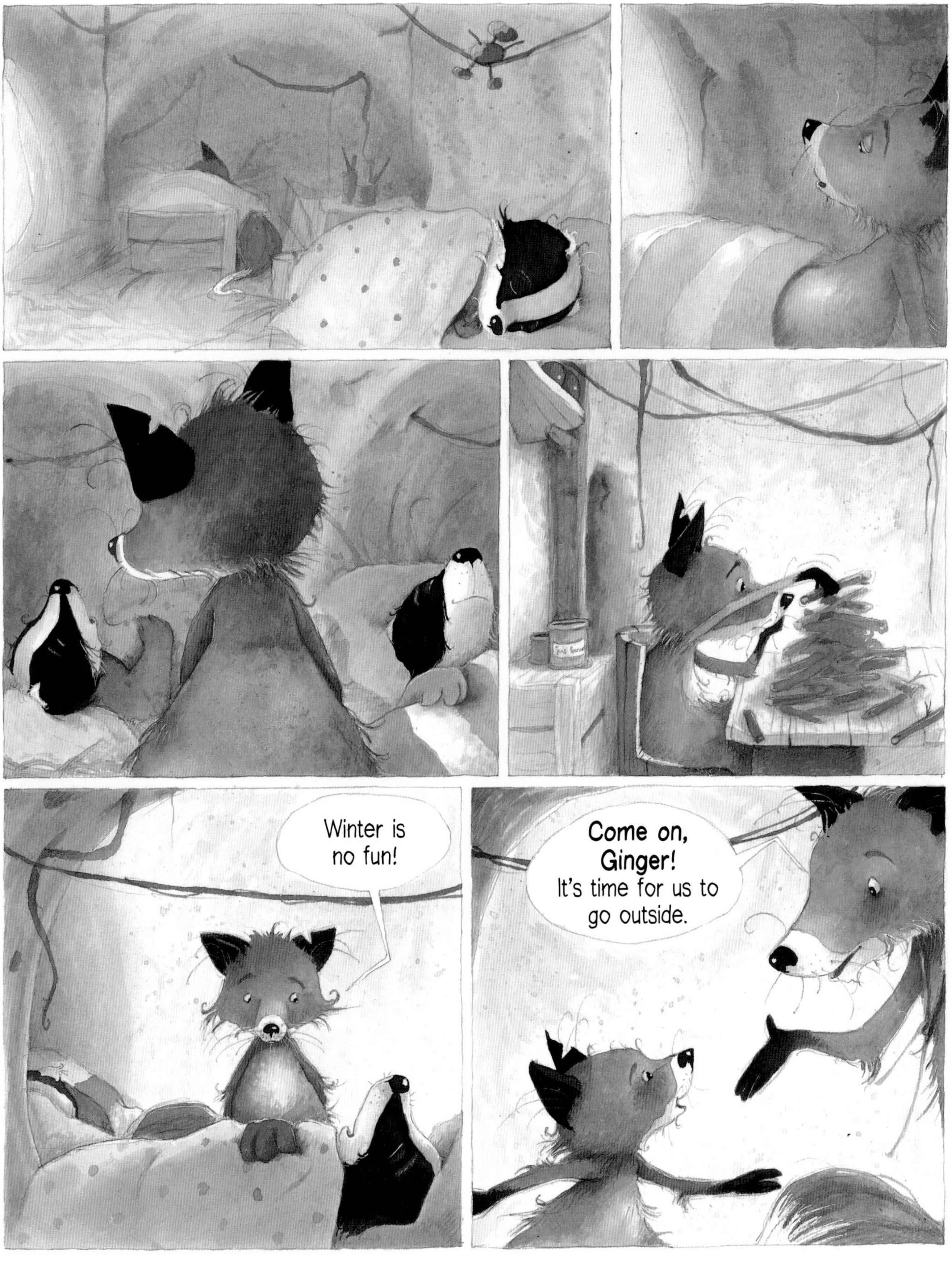
Winter is no fun!
Come on, Ginger! It's time for us to go outside.

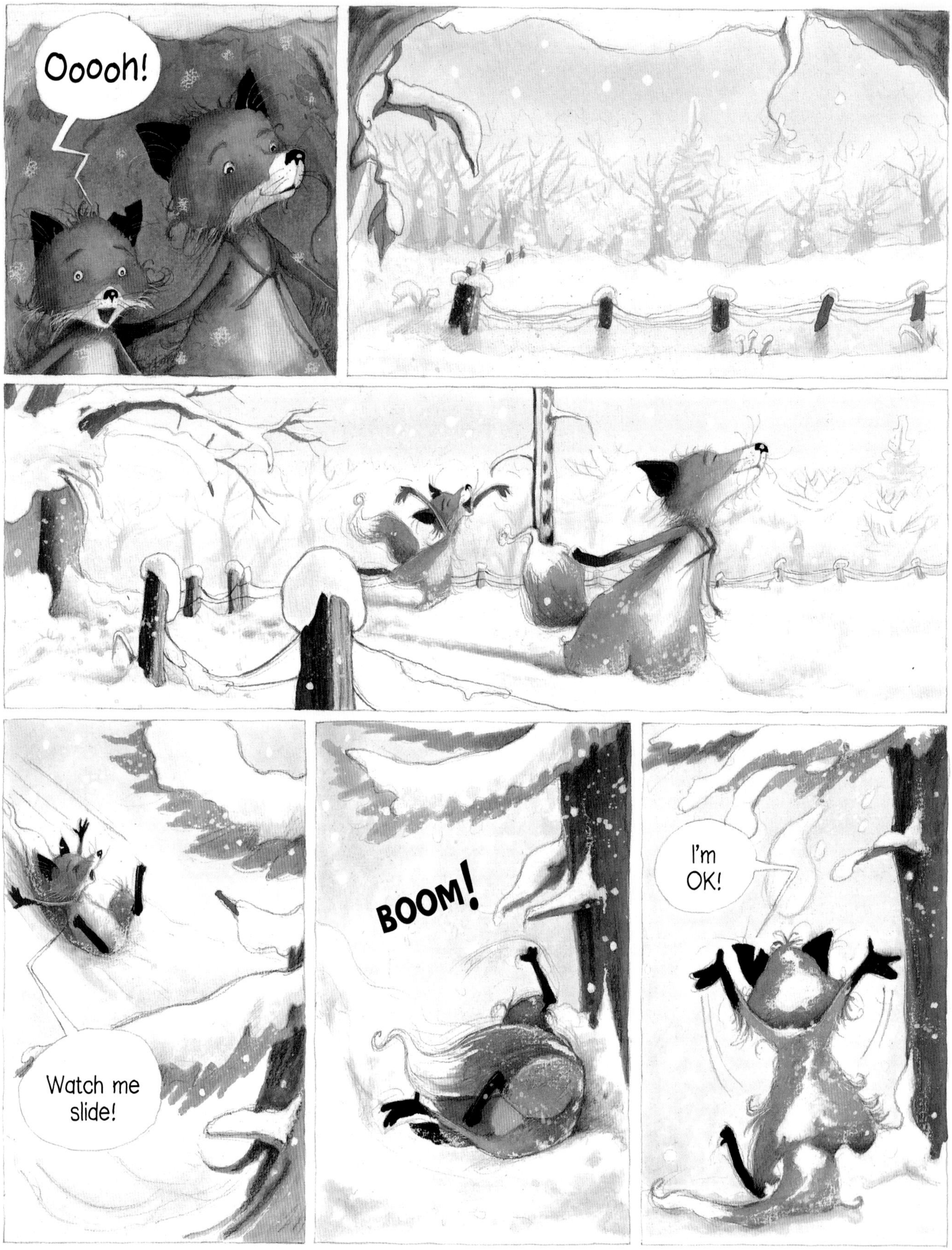
Ooooh!
Watch me slide!
BOOM!
I'm OK!

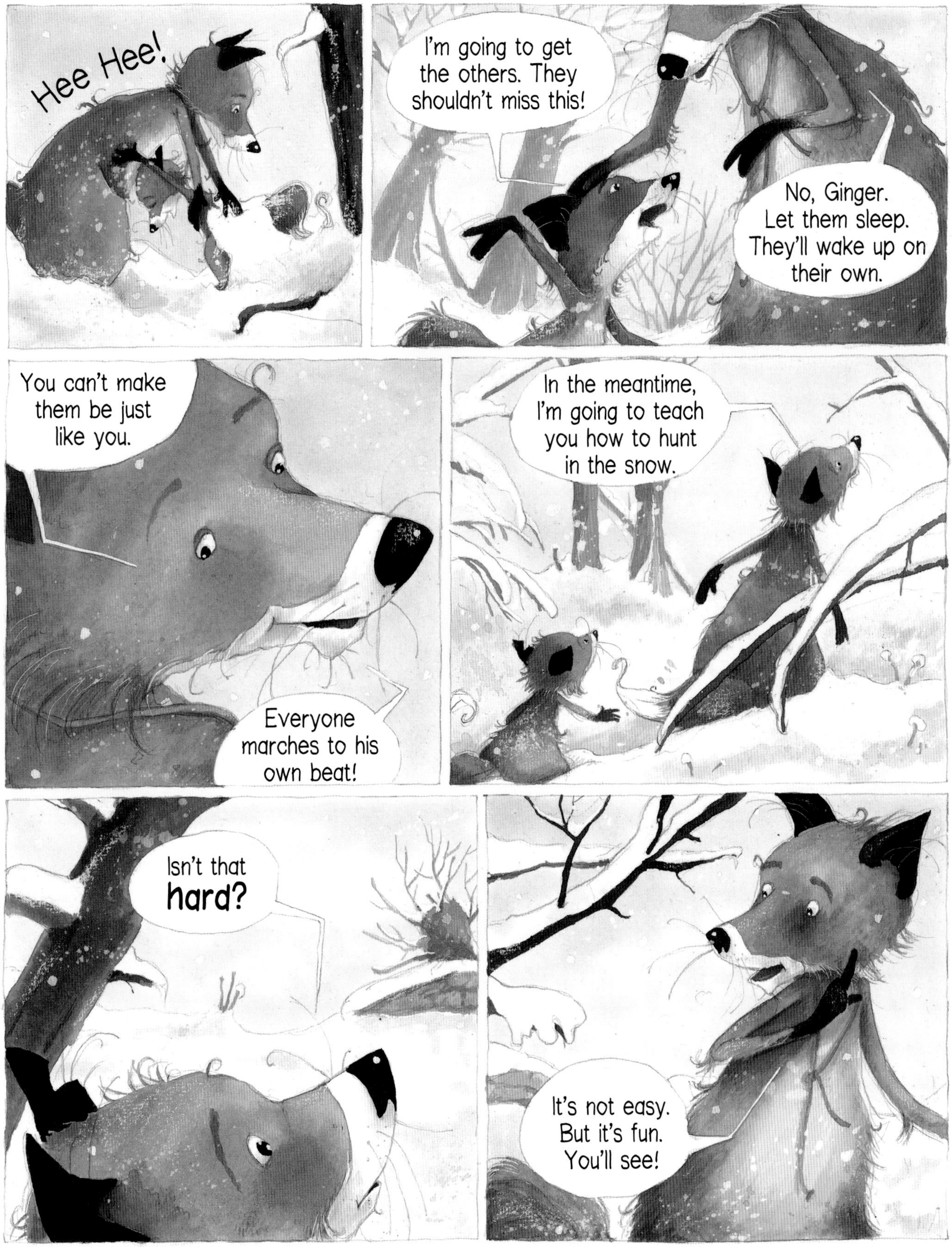
Hee Hee!
I'm going to get the others. They shouldn't miss this!
No, Ginger. Let them sleep. They'll wake up on their own.
You can't make them be just like you.
Everyone marches to his own beat!
In the meantime, I'm going to teach you how to hunt in the snow.
Isn't that **hard?**
It's not easy. But it's fun. You'll see!

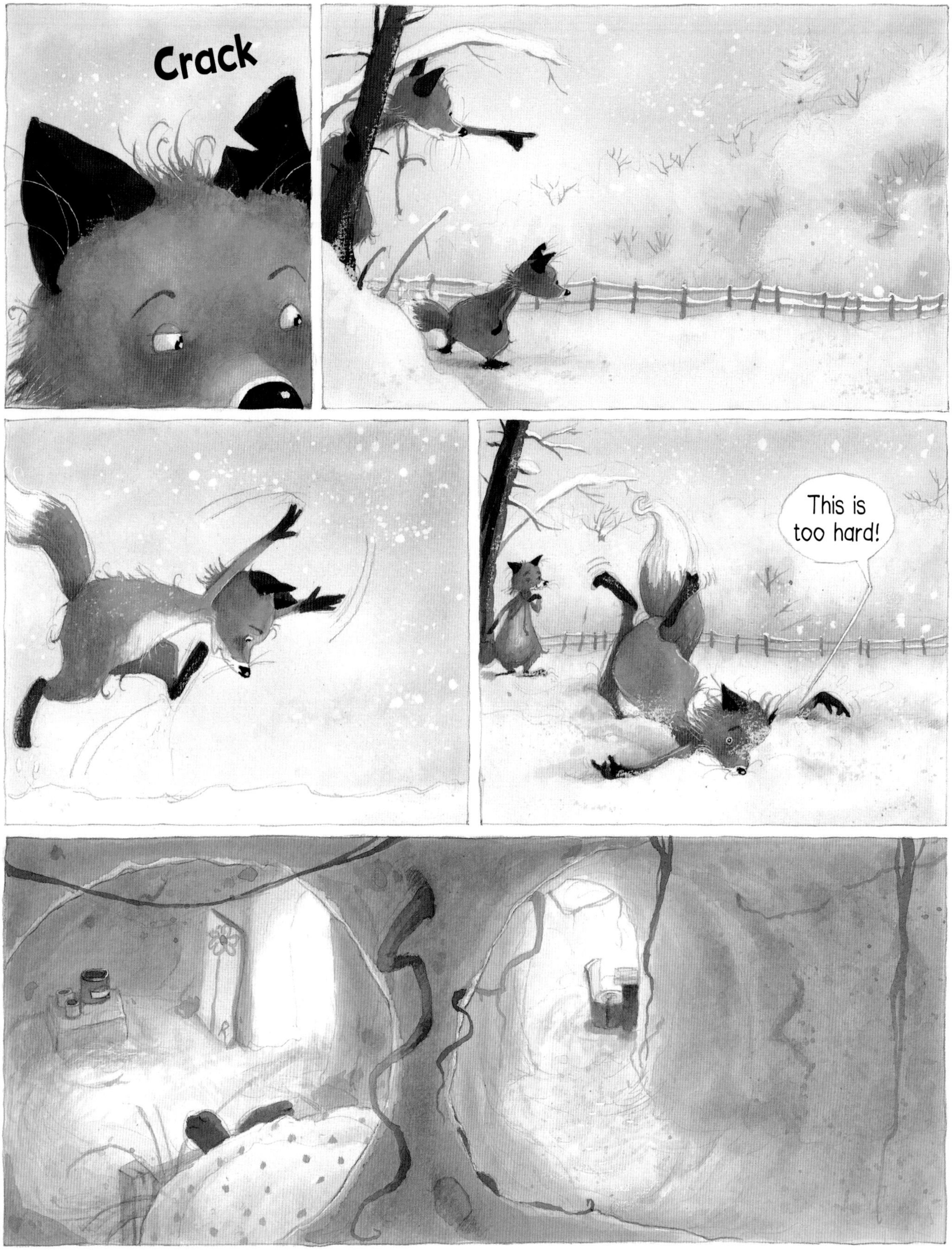
Crack
This is too hard!

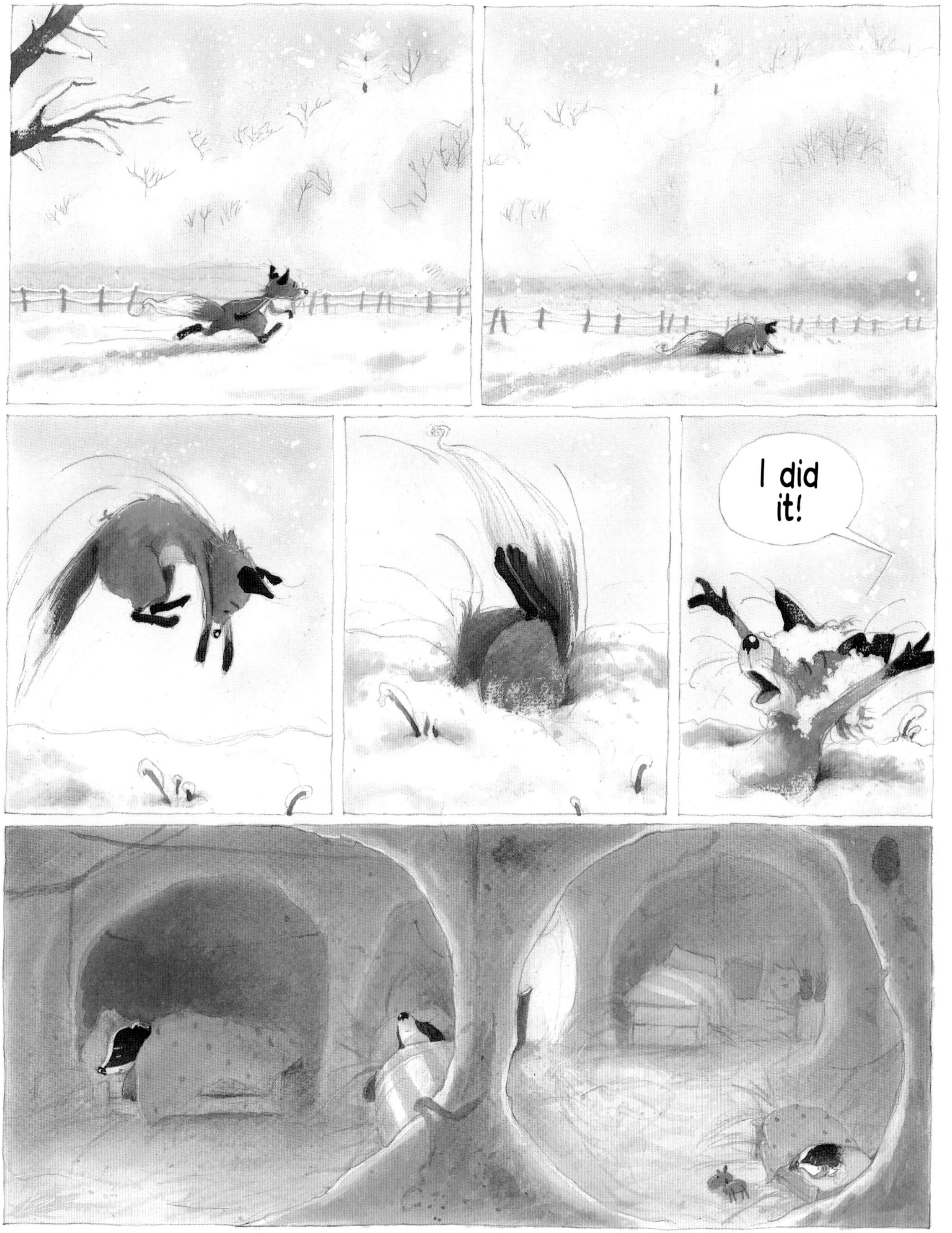
I did it!

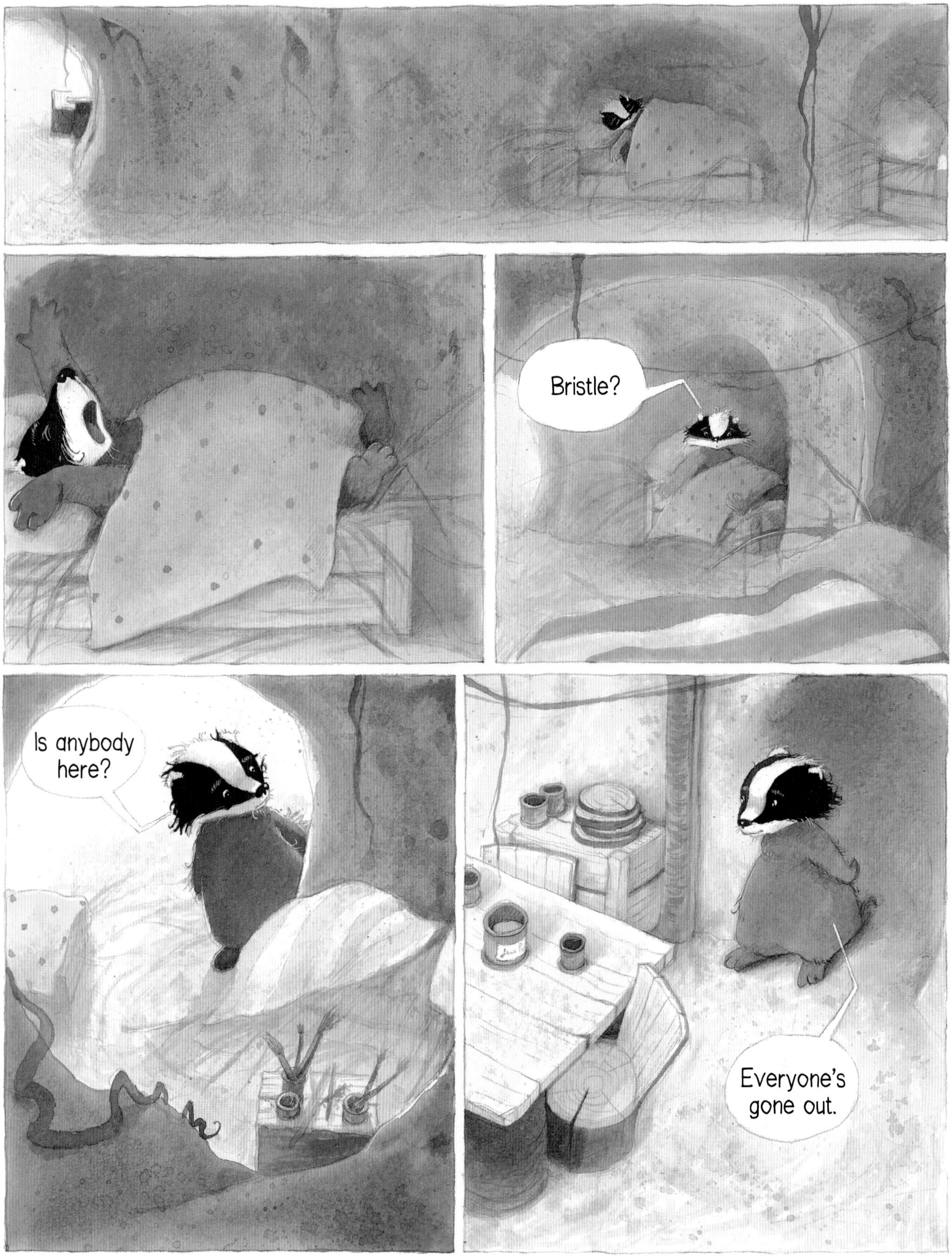
Bristle?
Is anybody here?
Everyone's gone out.

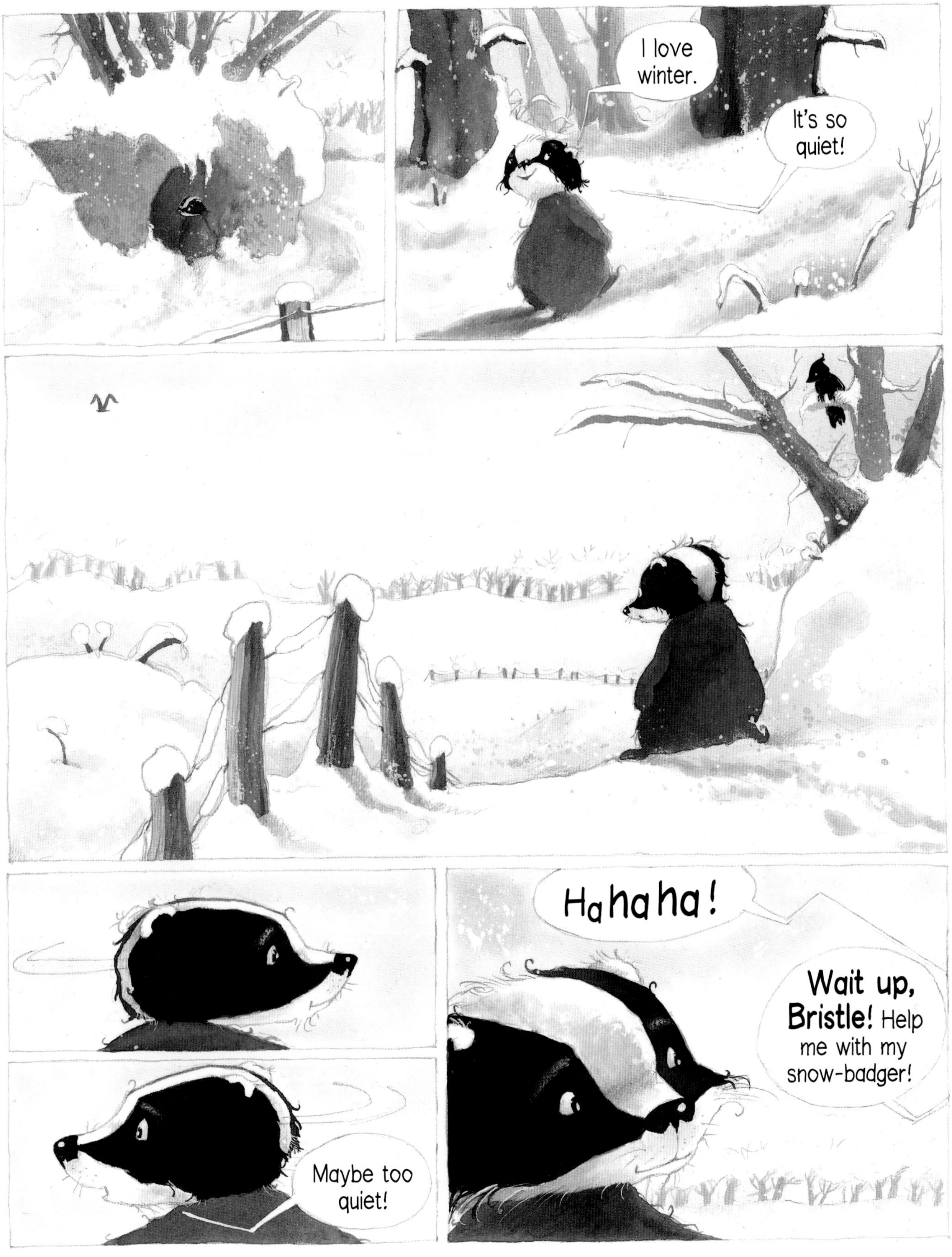
I love winter.
It's so quiet!
Maybe too quiet!
Hahaha!
Wait up, Bristle! Help me with my snow-badger!

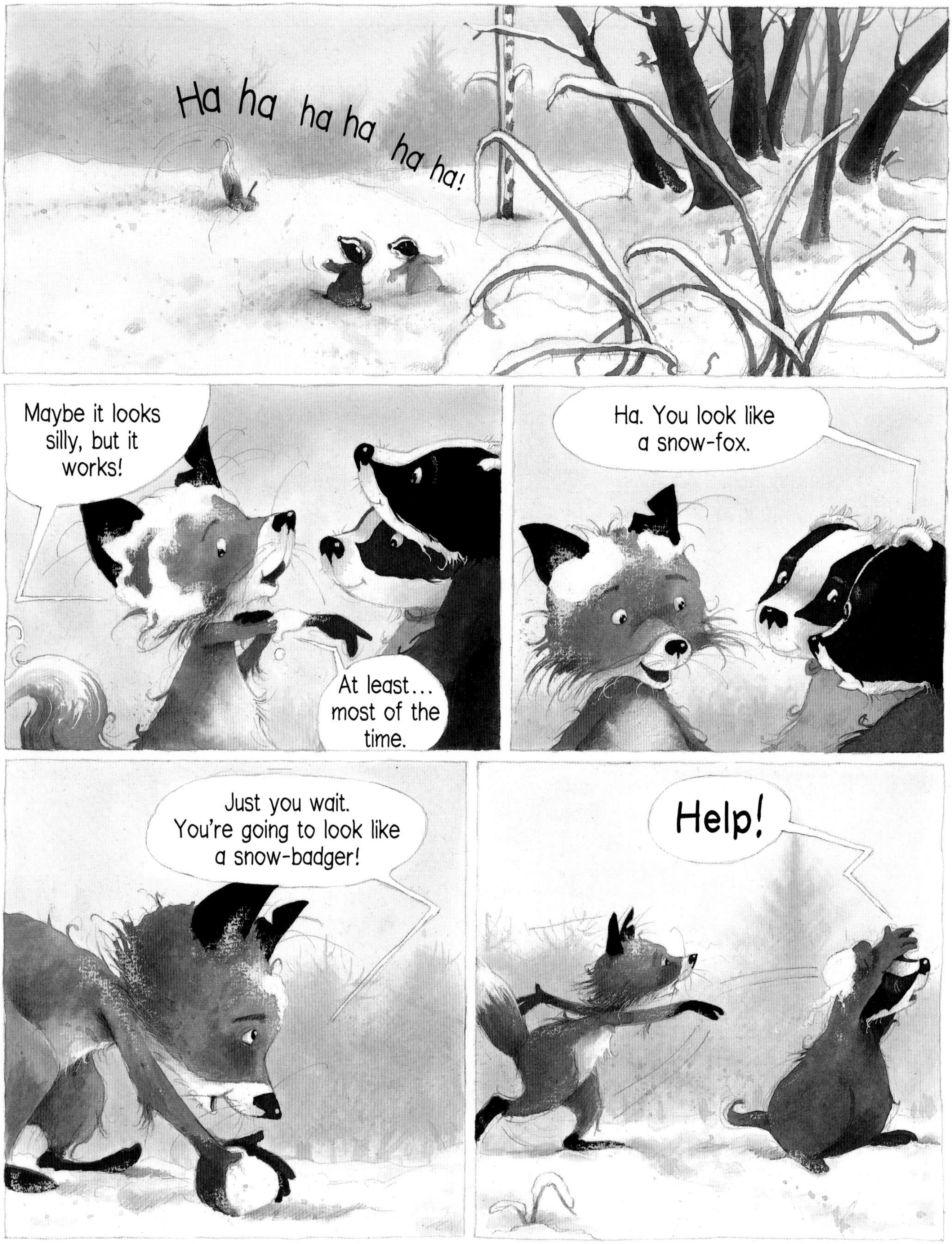
Ha ha ha ha ha ha!
Maybe it looks silly, but it works!
At least... most of the time.
Ha. You look like a snow-fox.
Just you wait. You're going to look like a snow-badger!
Help!

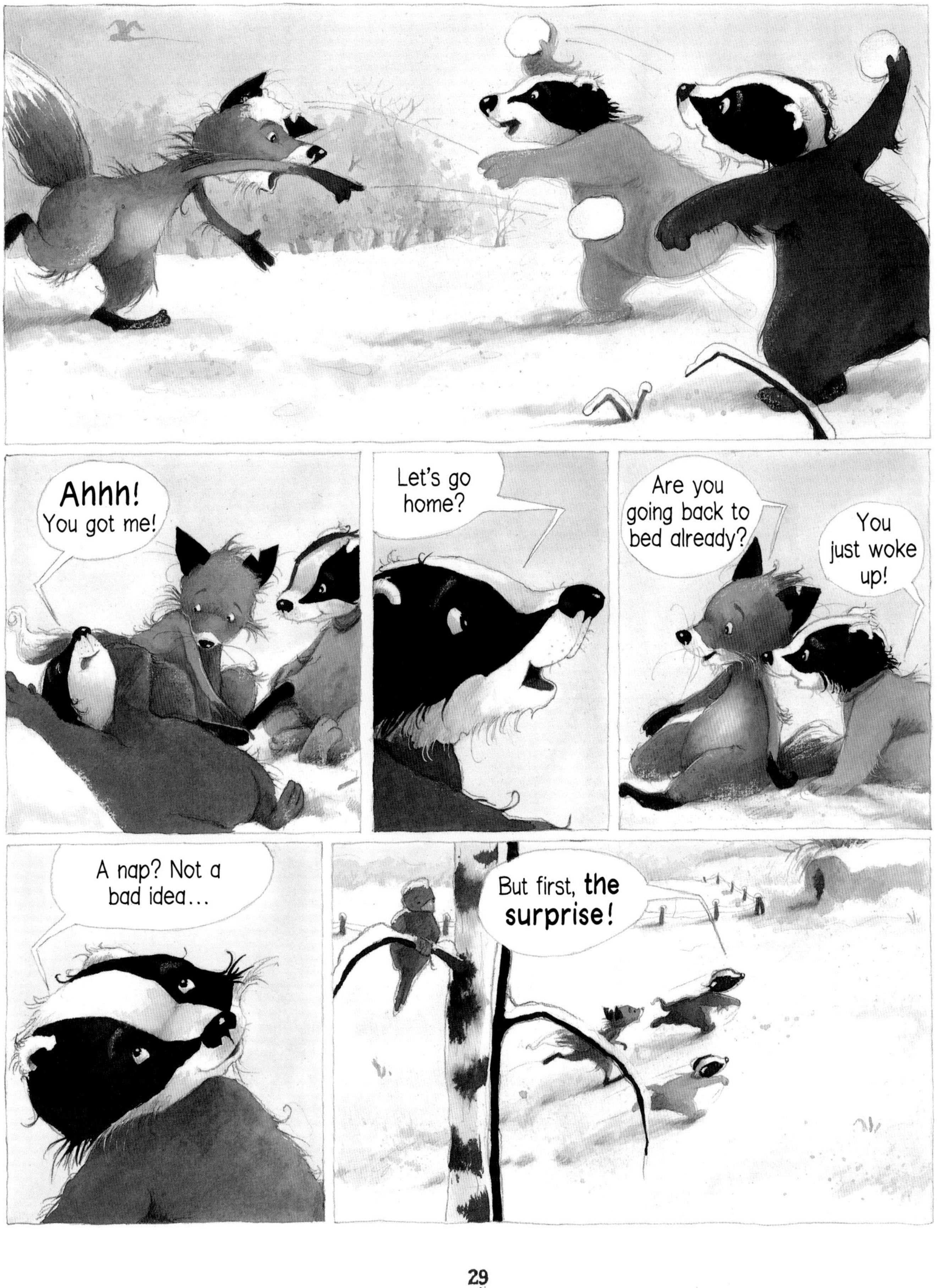
Ahhh! You got me!
Let's go home?
Are you going back to bed already?
You just woke up!
A nap? Not a bad idea...
But first, **the surprise!**

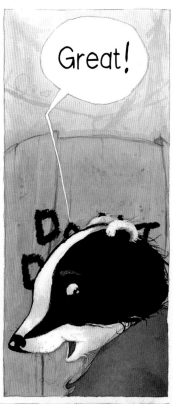

31

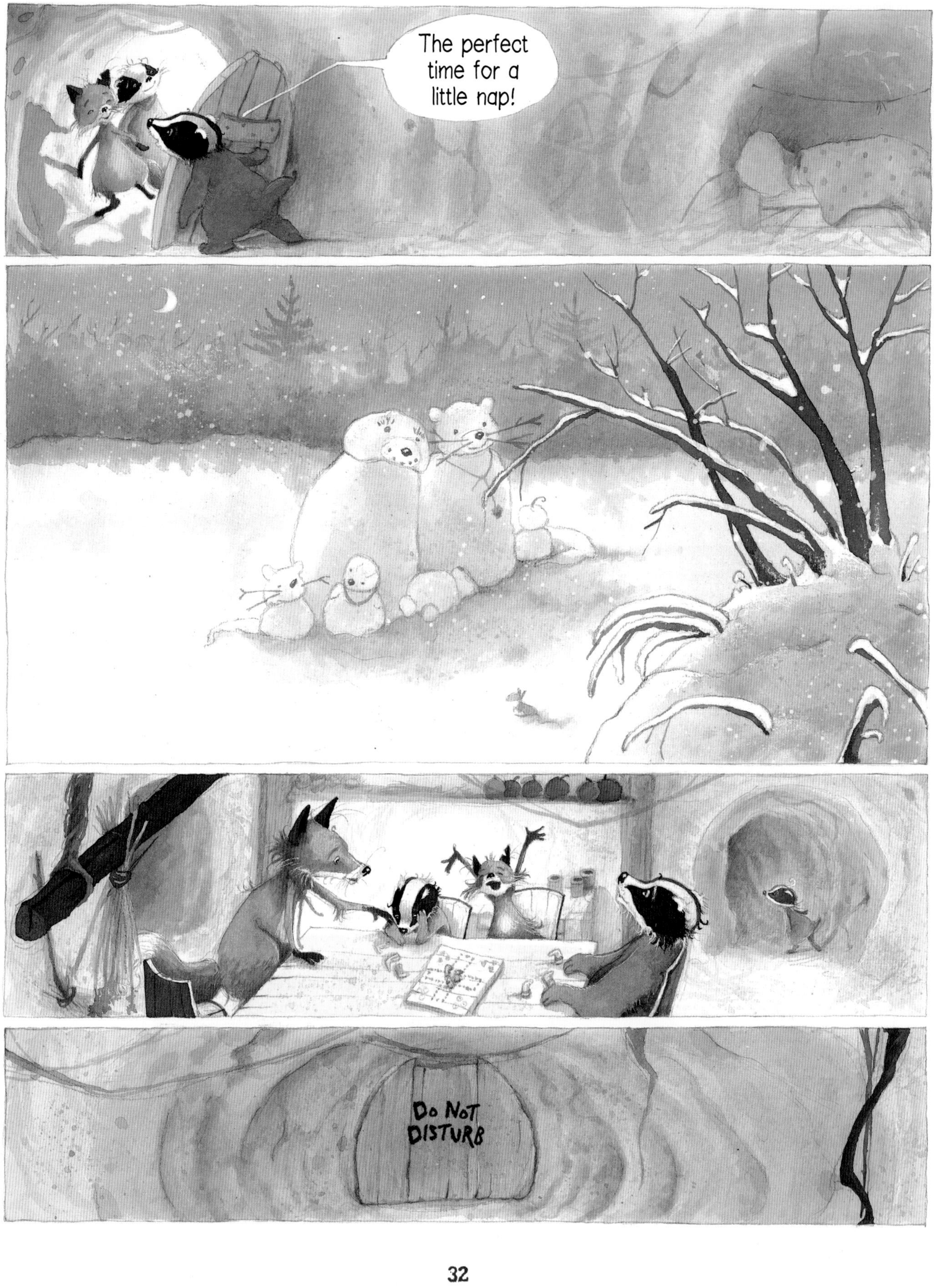
The perfect time for a little nap!
DO NOT DISTURB